LOST
BLOOD
& FAMILY

LOST BLOOD & FAMILY

ANIMELOVER21

Lost Blood & Family
Copyright © 2020 by animelover21. All rights reserved.

No part of this publication may be reproduced, stored in a retrieval system or transmitted in any way by any means, electronic, mechanical, photocopy, recording or otherwise without the prior permission of the author except as provided by USA copyright law.

The opinions expressed by the author are not necessarily those of URLink Print and Media.

1603 Capitol Ave., Suite 310 Cheyenne, Wyoming USA 82001
1-888-980-6523 | admin@urlinkpublishing.com

URLink Print and Media is committed to excellence in the publishing industry.

Book design copyright © 2020 by URLink Print and Media. All rights reserved.

Published in the United States of America

Library of Congress Control Number: 2020913225
ISBN 978-1-64753-440-0 (Paperback)
ISBN 978-1-64753-441-7 (Digital)

08.07.20

I knew I was different from other highschool kids but I would never have thought that I was that different until I transferred schools and had a counter with them on the day I was transferred there. My name is

James Seno. I am 18 years old and I am a student at Sora high until this afternoon. I was in class and the principal entered the classroom calling my name. Is James seno here? I raise my hand and say I'm here. He says to me I need you to come to my office. I say yes sir. The principal says to my home room teacher I will be taking him to my office. The teacher says ok go James. The principal says grab your stuff and come with me. I grab my stuff and head out of the classroom with him. As we are heading to his office he asks me how am i doing and how was my day i say everything is ok. He nods his head but has a worried look on his face. As we get close to his office and I see that there are cops at the doors in front of the Maine office I look at him and ask him what is going on as the officer walks up to us. He asks the principle is this the boy the principle says yes and says James go with this officer he needs to talk to you. I say ok and walk off with the officer he says i am officer jackson i need to tell you about your parents. I ask if something happened to them and he says i'll give you more detail when we get to the station. We head out of the school and to his car I ask him are they ok he looks away I ask him what happened he doesn't answer I say well Answer Me. We get to his car he says get in the back seat. I grab his shirt with tears in my eyes and ask one more time what happened as I'm sobbing he says get in the car. I let go of his shirt and get in the car as I'm whipping the tear off my face. He closes the door and heads to the driver's seat he gets in and puts on his seat belt. He starts the car and drives off. He asks if I need a tissue. I say no, I'm ok and look out the window. I go in my bag and pull out my phone and go to my pictures of me and my parents as i'm hoping they're ok. I'm scrolling through the pictures of me and my parents. I got a message from mom.Saying

James if you are getting this message me and dad are gone we are sorrie. The road ahead of you is going to be long and challenging but now we love you and kept you safe for as long as we could without telling the truth to protect you. I start crying again saying this can't be true mom what are saying i try to call her and it just rings the longer its rings the more despair sinks in. I hang up and try calling dad and it goes to voicemail. It feels as if my spirit is being drained from my body and as if there are no more tears to cry. We get to the station and the officer parks the car and says you can get out of the car. I ask shouldn't you take me to the moroge? He says the moroge is connected to the station and that's where I'm taking you know I just stand there. He says let's go and I follow him as we head to the moroge. I ask can you at least tell me how you found out that something happened to them. He says they were found at a park by a couple that was out jogging this morning. He says we're here and opens the door saying there are 2 detectives down these stairs they can tell you everything. I head down the stairs as I'm heading down the stairs. I start hearing a voice. I look behind me and look back in front and I don't see any one. I keep walking and I hear the voice again and its mom. I say mom is that you out loud. The voice answered saying yes my son it's me we don't have long i say i have so many questions. She says i know but listen there will be challenges you will face that will be hard and you will have to make a choice. The things we have been hiding from you will come to you and you will feel alone but you will not. You will meet some people that will forage your destiny. You will need to accept what will happen and what you see at the bottom of these stairs. You will need to find the courage to get through these hard times and challenges you will face. I hear dad's voice saying he will after all we did raise him as our own. I say what do you mean dad says we love you and remember you can do it. I reached the bottom of the stairs and I didn't hear their voices any more . I saw mom and dad on tables by each other's side. Their body's start to disappear as I am running to the tables they are on. I start yelling Dad Dad no no no this can't be happening don't leave me. I try talking to them saying what's happening to your bodies. Why are they disappearing? You really can't be dead please don't leave me. As the last of their bodies disappear i hear them say you will understand what's going soon and we will always be with you. We love you goodbye our beloved one. I fall on my knees lifeless as the 2 detectives come out the room behind me as they are talking and they turn and see me on my knees lifeless. They come up to me and ask me what happened to the body's i say they're gone. They say yea that's obvious what we are asking is what happened to them they can't just disappear. The doctor comes out behind them saying no that's what exactly happened and tells us to come into the room. The 2 detectives help me up and walk me to the room. They sit me in a chair and the detectives ask what did you mean by that doc. He says see here as he went to the computer screen that was connected to the camera that was showing the room we were just in before. He says look here as he rewinds the camera view to when i ran to the table dad was on and plays it from there. He says watch what happens to the bodies as he falls to his knees and cries. He starts to yell to his parents and they start to turn to ash and disappear as if they were waiting for him to come. They showed no signs of their body doing this until he got here. One detective said that's not possible for that to happen. People just don't turn to ash or just disappear. They can't wait for someone to come either when they're already gone so how is it possible for their bodies to do that? It's just not possible for human bodies to disappear or to turn to ash like that. The detective says we can deal with that later but we need to explain how his parents died to him. They turn and face me and introduce themselves to me. The first one says he is the head detective in this case his name is Jacob watson. The detective to his side is his partner Aaron Dotson. We will be looking into how your parents case. They were found in the park at 10am by a couple that was jogging by. They were attacking your by something that had claws but they also had their blood drained from their bodies. The marks they had where they were bit look like fangs though it was some DNA found by the person that attacked them. We sent this to the lab but it will take awhile for the result to come but we have some questions for you. As the detective is making sure that i understand what had happen to them his partners phone rings he walks out the room.I ask him what will happen to me he says we will put you in a foster home until they find you a family an you will still go to school i say i am being transfer though he say ok where to. In lakester high school it's a private school that wears a school uniform. He asks when do you start tomorrow. I say it is a livin dorm school. I need to move my stuff there. Officer Jackson say ok so sense its a live in we don't need to put in a foster home but we will need to talk to your school principal to let them know your situation that they need to update us if anything happens and you can contact us too if feel that weird people are showing up around you or if weird things that make you feel your in danger. I say ok i will and i ask if they need anything else before i leave so i could go get ready to be enrolled in my new school. I had to be there by 2pm to get my uniform for the school an to be debriefed on the rules of the school and its requirements for the class an the sports activities. They say that they will contact me if they do i say ok an leave the room to go back in the room where my parents where in . I walk to the table dad was on an put my hand on the surface an start rubbing thinking what did they mean when they said that to me an that they can't really be gone. As i'm daydreaming i hear my dad say be careful their will be people trying to get close to you, you will know who you can trust. By your throat felling dry your teeth aching and it will feel that you body is trying to morph or change if it does take the medicine we left for you in our room but if your blood goes cold that mean you need to get away. Before i can say anything the detective come behind me an say i'm sorry for your lost he says if anything happen please call an don't hesitate. I say thank you an walk past him to go up the stairs i look back at the tables an i think about what dad meant by that people will try to get close to me. I turned around to walk up the stairs i hear my mom say i know your dad said your we aren't you real parents that where you aunt and uncle but we loved you as our own son. When you meet your real parents and siblings try to understand why they gave you to us to keep you safe we love you James when you need to talk to us you will be able to you'll find a way bye our beloved James. i reach the top of the stairs an say bye mom and think of what she last said that i have siblings. Siblings that i don't know parents that i have parents gave me up to my aunt an uncle who raised has if i were their own. I had thought they were my real parents all of this is too much for me to process how I would i even find my parents and siblings I never met or known about until today. I decided i would think more about this tomorrow i catch the bus to the front of my house. I open the front gate an look in my bag for my keys to open the door .I take my keys out of my bag to open the door i go inside an close the door then i go straight up stairs to my parents room.Dad didn't tell me where they had left the medicine for me at in the room. I go to their room bathroom an look in the medicine cabinet to see a small box that has my name on it. I open it to see a note with 6 small white cap seals i open the note an read it says dear James this note tells you who you are and what kind of powers you have. You are part of a lost family that pure high breeds of lions an white fox's they were the most power of their kind which made them the enemy of pure high breed. That lead to their downfall you are the key to our revival an to end the darkness that has risen this medicine will help stop your transformation in public. We know your scared but it will make sense when you meet your birth family. You will be able to identify each other by your body reaction an their eyes when you meet a family member your eyes changes colors. They will change to golden-greyish do to you body trying to morph. If that happens if you don't have one of the cap seal go and hide or run an get it so you don't morph. They will be at laskers high that will be the only way you will be able to find them and get the answer you want. The note ends their i look at the medicine then close an put it in my bag i go to my room and pack my stuff so i'll be ready to be picked up to go to school. After i pack up it is 2 clock i hear a horn outside i go down stairs and put my shoes on an look around one more time before i leave thinking this will be the last time i will be in this house. I turn an open the door an leave before i do i lock the door an head to gate an open i look at house after i close the gate. I head to the car to get in the car an puts on my seat belt an the driver pulls off. As we are driving i am looking out of the window and think about what has happened and what my parents had said but mainly on why they were killed. I think why would anyone target them. What was the motive behind them getting killed but nothing came to me. Then i thought about my other parents and siblings that i have an don't know as i am the drive says we are at the school. I say oh already i say thank you and take my seat belt of an get out to close the door. He drives off and i look at the school it is huge school i think this school will be like another world but not knowing how other worldly it will be. I start walking toward the maine door of the school as i do i get knocked over by a girl when i opened my eyes i make eye contact with the girl on top of me. Her arms are on the side of me holding her up but when we meet eyes again my body starts to feel weird and painful has is it trying to change i start morn and cliche my body. So does the girl she falls on her back and we both start to roll back an forth but when do we lock eyes again an i see her eyes change gold-greyish she struggles an say you are my brother. As another girl comes an look at us. I look at her and she turns away immediately saying little sister is this him she says yes. I remember my parents saying what to do if this happens an get up to runway. The older sister grabs me an say wait i shake her off an run to the woods. As i think im clear i look in my bag for the medicine an see the box and open it to take it. I sit by a tree an think I'm clear but as soon as I do the 2 sisters pop up right in front of me saying we finally found you brother, auntie and uncle did a good job hiding you. I stand up with a surprised look on my face as i do the younger one kisses me on my lip and licks her after and then the older sister does the same after she does our body transform. Their eyes are grey-blueish with long silver and gold hair with long claws and their teeth are long like lion teeth but sharp like white foxes. I fall to the ground an say what happened to you 2 . she says i am Jasmine an pulls out a mirror that's on her make-up pouch and says you really are our brother and opens it. I look at it an i see me an say i look like you. Sasha hugs me an say brother brother i'm so happy we found you. I say wait wait what's going on. They both say we are your finances and sisters. I stand there an say no way my parents didn't say anything about that part what going on i mean aunt an uncle didn't tell me that they say come with us. I think what's going to happen to me and where we are going, and are we going to stay like this until we get to where we are going. Sasha says yes just until we get to principal office i say isn't that a bad thing for us to stay in form. Jasmine says that ok everyone else are already back at the dorms its 4 o'clock i say oh ok we reach the front door of the school and Sasha opens the door and we walk in and head to the office. I ask how old are they Jasmine says she's 19 and a senior just me and Sasha is 17 and she's a junior. I say oh ok and Sasha turns around, puts her back and says high big brother and smiles and turns around and continues walking until we reach the office. Jasmine opens the door saying mom,dad are you here. I hear a female voice as we walk in. Saying your girls are finally her and lookups from her voice send a shock down my back. She asks Jasmine why she is in her form and Jasmine looks towards me and immediately tears start to fill her eyes and she says James James your James arent you and runs to and hugs me. Saying James James you're finally back to us. I say mom she moves back and says yes yes it me as she's transformed. I look at her and my head feels as if splitting and I put my hand on my head and I fall on one knee and a flood of memories come back like a flood gate had been opened. When it finished I saw my mom in front me and my sisters on their knees on the side of me with their hands on my back.I say mom mom with tears in my eyes and I look towards my sisters calling their name Jasmine,Sasha and hug them saying im back.and we all cry.

Mom says get up and lead me to the couch holding my hand.I sit down and she's on her knee in front of me as my sisters are on the other sides. I look at Sasha and you have grown in the 10 years I have not been around. She laughs and says big brother big brother you're finally back i have missed you. She goes in her pocket and takes out a key chain and says do you remember this i grab it and say you still have this i gave it to you for your birthday the day before i left she says that's right dad had carried me away after you did and i never seen you after that i have alway been worried about you. I smile at her and say know I'm back you don't have to know. Then I look over to Jasmine and smile as she wipes her tears away. I say come know this isn't the big sister I have alway looked up to and I don't remember you being a crybaby. She looks at me and says but… it's so hard without you around. I have been lost without you. All you used to do is follow me around saying sissy sissy and all of sudden you were gone as if you were never there. Mom put her head down and said I'm sorry i.. We had to send him away to my brother and sister and whip his memories or we would have been in trouble. Our kind is a threat to the others so if they felt that we were becoming a threat they would eliminate us. I remember being the first male being born in 200 hundred years. I can revive our lineage of pure high breeds. Jasmine says right in order for our family to activate our power we have to have siblings that are 2 girls and one male and they have to be wedded to activate our full power. You remember when we kissed you I said I know this part the 3 of us can only transform we kiss but when we wed it shows the proof of our bound and feeling for each other. That's when dad walks in he says James with a shocked look on his face. I tell his dad how you smile at him and get up and run to him and give a hug he let go of the dog and says James James your back. I say we no longer have to be in hiding any more. I got my powers and we can be together without fear. I say but what are we going to do about the other families, the ones that's been managing us to make sure we don't revive. The Panguars and Tigardess Mom said to call all the students to the gym we're going to have you 3 take you animal forms dad said good idea. I had asked about our servant the lipardess and the leoponess .Jasmine said the leoponess stayed loyal and waited for your return but the lipardess went into hiding. I say our eyes left but the ears stayed. I say no way no way Luna would not abandon us like that. Sasha says she lost hope of your return and is trying to keep the remaining leopardess alive. Lilla always knew you would come back and was at this school. I say so what aboutLigaress and the Jagpards are they still with us.

Mom smiles and says you'll see and dad cut's in saying all students are heading to the gym. Mom says let's get going. I say ok and we head out to the gym. We reach the gym and I see a whole bunch of students lined up facing the stage as we are walking pace them. Me ,Dad,Jasmine,and Sasha stand to the side as mom goes to the make and starts speaking I am sorry for calling you back here but we are going to show the student body something now come to you 3.

Know you all know these my daughters Jasmine and Sasha as for this young mane well you just gonna have to wait until the end for you to know Jasmine and Sasha you may start. They both blush and Jasmine goes first and kiss James and transfor her eyes change to a grey_bluish color with long teeth that are shard as white fox with claw and her hair is silver-goldish color Sasha goes next and her and James transform at the and there appearance mathes Jasmines.

The students Gasp saying how how is this possible one of the student say no no it be and mom says know you 3 and we transform into our trues form and as soon as they James is recognized by the 4 other families that are severant Lilla ,Luna,Ashley,and Leon come to the front and says James you are back. I who are you out of the 4 of you I can only recognize one of you and that is Lilla of the Lipardess she transforms into her true form and bow her head.My master James you are finally back i knew you would be and give a row to show respect. I say yes you may come up and she says yes my lord and jumps up on the stage and gets behind me. I say know who are you 3. One says know James their now way you forgot who i am as she bows in her human form i hear a ring i say wait you...are. She says finally you dunder head and transform i say Ashley is that you. She says well are you going to invite me up to the stage? I say of course come on you know you're always welcomed and she bows her head and comes up. Next the boy goes he says i am Leon you may not remember me you save me once when we were younger i say i did. He says i was still in my cub form when you so you might not remember me. He transforms and when he does i see a scare on his leg i say ah you're from that time yes yes I remember. He bowed his head and yes lord i am i may be young but i will protect you i say mhmm you may come up. I say know you are the last one She stands there holding her arm with a dark expression i say well you are. She transforms and says did you really forget me and says my lord can we have dohyo. I say Dohyo do you want to be free that much she says no my lord but if you have forgotten me then i rather be free. I sense a great sadness in her words. I say ok let's have a dohyo I say you do know what kind of pure breed i am right. She says my lord i say i can tell you're a

Leopardess i thought you guys were in hiding. She if you will know everything. I say you determined i see i ask mom can you give the signal she says yes i say ok and i ask the lipardess what form would she like to use she says our true form i ok and i think in my head why would invoke a battle especially in our true form when she clearly know the outcome. I say mom and she says know dohyo we stare at each other as i'm looking in her eyes or light blue yes i start to feel as if they are famiralar and she attack i snap out of it and dodge she come back for and i go under her to flip her when i see a scar on her stomach when i go to grapple to flip her she reverses is and i call he name i say Luna is that you she lays are head on my chest and says James James your back your back i lets get up when we do she rubs her head against mines and i say you really are Luna. She says how dare you just leave like that you know i am only loyal to you. I say let's go to the stage. She bows to me and we get on stage. I say the 4 generals of the White Lion are assembled. Let it be known I am reviving the pure breed of the white lions.

www.ingramcontent.com/pod-product-compliance
Lightning Source LLC
LaVergne TN
LVHW021739060526
838200LV00052B/3367